The CATS Who like BATS

Written by
Helen Dhue

Illustrated by
Julia Lopresti

On an island in the middle of the sea
There was a town that was full of kitties

And the town was a place where the cats got along
They liked to drink milkshakes and play cat ping-pong

The cats had fish feasts and time in the sun

Life on cat island was really quite fun

However, the cats didn't always play nicely

In fact, there was one animal they hated precisely

The cats disliked bats. How this started we don't know
But the disdain for bats started a long time ago
On the island of cats mean rumors had started
The way cats spoke of bats was very mean-hearted

One night on this island far away
A group of cats on an evening in May
were enjoying a summer night in the park
and drinking milkshakes by a fire in the dark

The cats were sitting down and telling stories
They told tales of the island and all of its glories

However, the subject of the stories started to stray
As one cat told a story in a very mean way

"I have a story to tell," one cat said,

'it's a story about a creature that hides under your bed!"

"Bats," the cat shrieked, "are really quite scary,

They are like birds, but ugly and hairy."

Another cat chimed in, "I've heard that too,
I've also heard that bats never use shampoo!
So they fly around and make things smell bad"
The cats hated things dirty so that story made them mad.

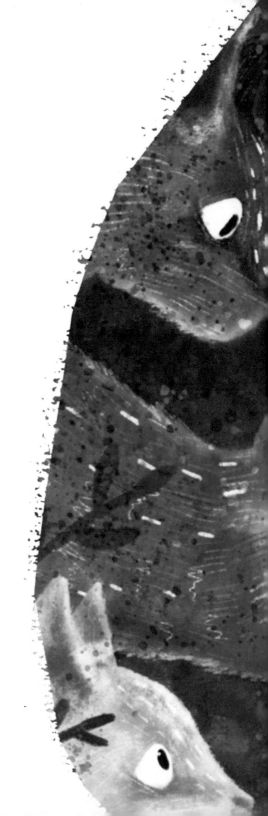

The cats continued to tell stories and sit around
When all of the sudden they heard an odd sound
the strangest of creatures had fallen to the ground!

Little did the cats know things would change that night
but in the moment the cats were full of fright

The cats surrounded the tiny thing-
It looked like a cat, but smaller, with wings

"OH NO! IT'S A BAT,"

one cat screamed.
"Look at him, I bet he
has never been clean!"

The bat was shaken and wanted to cry
and before he spoke, wiped the tear from his eye.

Despite his fear, he used a brave voice
"I may not be clean now, but it wasn't my choice!

I've been flying for days and I'm as tired as can be
I flew to this island in search of a tree.
My family and I need somewhere to stay,
as our home is so far away!"

One cat said, "Sure, you little bean,
maybe you're usually pretty darn clean."
And the cat continued with his bad attitude,
"but don't you bats only eat stinky food?
And I'm sorry but we can't have that here
where our milk is so sweet and our water's so clear."

"I don't know where you heard that our food is so gross,
I like to eat apples and strawberry toast!
Plus," the bat added with pride and glee,
"some bats eat fruits and others like fleas.
There are so many different kinds of bats,
only some eat bugs and others don't eat like that!"
The bat continued saying, "even so, eating bugs is fine too,
one of my favorite dishes happens to be June beetle stew,
food is not gross just because someone eats differently than you."

"Well, fruits do sound yummy," one cat said,

"And June beetle stew sounds delicious with some bread!"

But another cat was still shaking his head.
"I don't want bats on this island. It's only for us,
I'm tired of other animals making a fuss.
Us cats have been on this island for years,
The island is ours. Us cats belong here."

"Actually, this island is not ours,"
a little cat muttered under the stars.
"Before us," the cat said, "you know what was here?
This island had belonged to the deer.
And yes, many deer are still around
But we took a large part of their ground
So I don't think we have the right to say
Who has to go and who gets to stay."

So, maybe it would be alright

If we let the bat and his family spend the night."

The cats started to nod their heads and agree.
"Maybe we should welcome this bat family,
We want to make up for what we have said."
So, the cats helped the bats find a nice bed.

By the time the cats found a spot for the bats to stay,
The night was gone, and it was day

This happened to be perfect for the bats,
as their sleeping schedule was similar to the cats.

"We sleep when it's light out,"
the bat explained

"We like the dark, too,"
one cat proclaimed.

"Maybe bats aren't scary after all,"
another cat had spoken
And something in the cats that day
was awoken.

The cats enjoyed the bats in their short, little stay.

When it was time for the bats to be on their way
One of the cats said, "my bat friend dear,
Me and the other cats, well we like you guys here,

We are sorry about the stories we told about you,

We are sorry we said things that weren't even true.

If you can forgive us for the lies that we told

we would love for your family to make a household,

right here on this island, we'd love your presence"

And the bat responded without hesitance,

"At first I thought you cats were mean,

But after our time here, I have seen,

That we are actually quite alike,

We like the night and fruits and bikes.

But we are also different and that is good too,

Maybe one day you can try some June beetle stew!

And we would like to live with you guys,

Thank you for this pleasant surprise."

Things changed on the island that day

And life on the island has been better that way

The cats taught the bats how to make milkshakes

And the bats taught the cats how to make fruitcakes

The bats taught the cats how to hang upside down

And the cats loved having the bats around.

And today on the island you'll find many bats.

And the animals on the island...

Well, they like it like that.

ABOUT THE STORY

When I was about four years old I told a story to my mother who typed it down. During the pandemic, I was looking through my childhood artwork and stumbled upon "The Cats That Like Bats." I decided to rewrite the story and ask my good friend Julia Lopresti to do the artwork for the book. I'm very grateful to have so many supportive people help me with the process of creating this book. A huge thanks to my mother, father, and sister who have always supported my creative endeavors, Dr. Krystyn Moon for guiding me in the creation of my website www.catswholikebats.com, Emily Fang for her editing skills, and Julia Lopresti for bringing this book to life with her wonderful artwork.

CPSIA information can be obtained
at www.ICGtesting.com
Printed in the USA
BVRC090437070921
616200BV00005BA/17